BATMAN

THE BRAVE AND THE BOLD ™

Written by Tracey West
Illustrated by Dan Panosian
Batman created by Bob Kane

Grosset & Dunlap
An Imprint of Penguin Group (USA) Inc.

NIGHT OF THE MUMMY

GROSSET & DUNLAP
Published by the Penguin Group
Penguin Group (USA) Inc., 375 Hudson Street, New York, New York 10014, USA
Penguin Group (Canada), 90 Eglinton Avenue East, Suite 700,
Toronto, Ontario M4P 2Y3, Canada
(a division of Pearson Penguin Canada Inc.)
Penguin Books Ltd., 80 Strand, London WC2R ORL, England
Penguin Group Ireland, 25 St. Stephen's Green, Dublin 2, Ireland
(a division of Penguin Books Ltd.)
Penguin Group (Australia), 250 Camberwell Road,
Camberwell, Victoria 3124, Australia
(a division of Pearson Australia Group Pty. Ltd.)
Penguin Books India Pvt. Ltd., 11 Community Centre, Panchsheel Park,
New Delhi–110 017, India
Penguin Group (NZ), 67 Apollo Drive, Rosedale,
North Shore 0632, New Zealand
(a division of Pearson New Zealand Ltd.)
Penguin Books (South Africa) (Pty.) Ltd., 24 Sturdee Avenue,
Rosebank, Johannesburg 2196, South Africa

Penguin Books Ltd., Registered Offices:
80 Strand, London WC2R ORL, England

The publisher does not have any control over and does not assume any
responsibility for author or third-party websites or their content.

BATMAN and all related names, characters, and elements
are trademarks of DC Comics © 2010. All rights reserved. Published by
Grosset & Dunlap, a division of Penguin Young Readers Group,
345 Hudson Street, New York, New York 10014. GROSSET & DUNLAP is a
trademark of Penguin Group (USA) Inc. Printed in the U.S.A.

Library of Congress Control Number: 2009023046

ISBN 978-0-448-45339-2   10 9 8 7 6 5 4 3 2 1

"This is the best game yet!" said Fun Haus with glee. "I'll turn these Tickle the Teddy Bear toys into the cutest bunch of bank robbers ever!"

Fun Haus looked like a crazed court jester. The villain wore a bright yellow costume with purple gloves and boots. Bells hung from his purple jester's hat, and two bright red circles were painted on his cheeks.

He stood on a platform overlooking his hideout. The place looked like an indoor carnival. Bright lights hung from the ceiling, carnival game stands were lined up against the wall, and a small Ferris wheel spun around and around behind Fun Haus.

The villain was smiling down at a line of fluffy, pink teddy bears traveling down a

conveyor belt. At the end of the belt, the teddy bears fell one by one into a large steel bin.

Bam! The factory door slammed open. Batman and Green Arrow appeared in the open doorway.

"Game's over, Fun Haus," Batman said. "You and your terrible toys aren't going to be robbing any banks today."

Fun Haus's grin turned upside down. "Batman! You're always spoiling my fun!"

"There's nothing fun about crime, Fun Haus," Batman replied.

Green Arrow shook his head. "Are you serious, Bats? You brought me here to battle a clown and a bunch of teddy bears? I have better things to do."

Batman's friend and fellow hero wore a green vest and tights, like Robin Hood. A black mask covered his eyes, and a bow and quiver of arrows were strapped to his back.

"Well, if you insist on staying, you can at least play by the rules," Fun Haus called out. "Let's *spin* to see who goes first!"

Fun Haus pressed a green, glowing gem on his purple belt. The Ferris wheel hopped off of its base and zoomed down the warehouse, aiming right for Batman and Green Arrow!

The two heroes jumped out of the way just in time. The Ferris wheel slammed into the wall and exploded in a shower of sparks.

Green Arrow loaded an arrow into his bow and aimed it at Fun Haus. However, the bright warehouse suddenly plunged into darkness.

Fun Haus's eerie voice echoed around the warehouse. "You can't catch me!" he taunted.

Green Arrow sighed. "This guy is starting to get on my nerves."

"Then let's stop him," Batman said.

"Right," Green Arrow said. "This Illumination Arrow should do the trick."

Green Arrow put a different arrow into his bow and aimed it at the ceiling.

Bam! There was a small explosion, and the warehouse flooded with yellow light. The heroes could now see that a row of pink teddy bears stood in front of them.

"*Do you want to play with us?*" the teddy bears asked.

They didn't wait for an answer. Their eyes began to glow red.

"I'm on it," Batman said.

He lunged to the side and threw a Batarang at the line of teddy bears. The sharp weapon sliced through the toys one by one, chopping off each bear's head. The last teddy bear managed to shoot off a laser blast from its eyes before the Batarang reached it. Luckily, the blast ricocheted off the wall and hit a metal toy bin.

Another army of bears marched toward them from the other side. Green Arrow quickly shot an arrow bomb at them.

Boom! Bits of pink fluff rained down on the warehouse floor.

"You're not playing fair!" Fun Haus wailed.

The criminal stood on top of a large bin of colored balls. He pressed another gem on his belt and one wall of the bin fell open, sending the balls sprawling on the ground.

Pop! Pop! Pop! Each ball was a small bomb. Batman quickly shot a grappling

hook onto a steel ceiling beam. He grabbed Green Arrow by the arm and pulled them both up off of the floor.

Down below, Fun Haus was racing for the door. Batman took a shooter off his utility belt and shot out a net. It landed on top of Fun Haus, knocking him down.

Zip! Zip! Zip! Zip! Green Arrow shot an arrow into each corner of the net, pinning Fun Haus inside.

Batman and Green Arrow jumped down to the floor.

"Looks like the score is heroes, one, Fun Haus, zero," Green Arrow joked.

Batman heard a beeping sound inside his helmet. A message was coming through, and Batman listened.

"I've got to go," Batman told Green Arrow. "Think you can wrap this up?"

Green Arrow grinned. "I'll even put a nice bow on it."

Batman nodded. He had to hurry.

His old friend the Atom needed his help.

CHAPTER TWO

"Thanks for coming so quickly, Batman."

Dr. Ryan Choi stood up from his desk in his science lab. When he wasn't in costume as the hero the Atom, Ryan wore a white lab coat over his regular clothes. He had smooth, dark hair and intelligent, brown eyes.

"You said a friend of yours is in trouble," Batman said.

Ryan walked to a computer monitor and quickly typed on the keyboard. The image of a young man with wavy, black hair appeared.

"This man is Larry Rodriguez. Larry and I attended college together. We both wanted to be scientists," Ryan explained. "We became friendly even though I went on to study astrophysics, and Larry went on to become an archaeologist."

Batman nodded. "So what happened to Larry?"

Ryan pressed another button. "Last week, I received this video message from him."

A video popped up on the monitor. Larry was inside what looked like a trailer, with books piled up behind him and maps on the walls. He was sweating, and he looked terrified.

"Ryan, when I started this dig, I thought it was going to be great—the high point of my career," Larry said. "But now I'm not so sure. We've found the tomb of a guy named Ombos. From what we can tell, he was an Egyptian priest. Our hieroglyph translator read some kind of warning on the outside of the tomb. It said we'd be cursed if we opened it, but I didn't believe it."

Larry nervously ran a hand through his hair. "But now I'm not so sure. Strange things have been happening. Equipment disappears and then shows up out of nowhere. I'm starting to think maybe the curse is real after all."

Ryan paused the video. "I was not concerned after receiving this message. The belief in curses is not logical. I assumed the stress of the work was affecting Larry's brain chemistry," he told Batman. "However, Larry's next message is a different matter."

Ryan fast-forwarded the video. Larry's face appeared again. It was dark, and he was outside. Batman could see the mouth of a cave behind Larry—the entrance of the tomb of Ombos.

"Ryan, I know you probably think I'm imagining things, but you've got to believe me," Larry said. He sounded desperate. "This tomb is definitely cursed. There was an accident today. One of my assistants was climbing down into the tomb, and the ladder snapped. Luckily, he wasn't hurt too badly, but it could have been worse. I'm afraid that—*Aaaaaaaaah*!"

Larry's voice turned into a scream as a thick, purple fog appeared out of nowhere, surrounding him. Then the tape turned to static and went blank.

"I still do not believe the tomb is cursed—but I do believe Larry is in danger," Ryan said. "I suspect a super-villain is behind this."

Batman nodded. "That's what this looks like. And I have an idea who it might be."

"So do I," Ryan said. He rewound the video, then pressed some buttons to zoom in on one spot in the purple fog. As the image got larger, the face of a grinning skull came into view. The skull was attached to a walking stick.

"Exactly," Batman said. "This is the work of Gentleman Ghost!"

CHAPTER
THREE

The morning sun streaked the desert floor with red and gold. Batman's jet cast a shadow over the sand as it sped toward a small chain of reddish brown hills.

"If the coordinates Larry gave us are right, the tomb of Ombos should be right below us," Batman said. "I'm going in for a landing."

Ryan nodded from the passenger seat. The jet swooped down and made a smooth landing in front of the hills. Batman and Ryan climbed out of the craft.

"That appears to be Larry's trailer," Ryan said, pointing.

They walked to the long, white trailer and stepped inside. It was still full of equipment, but there was no sign of life. Ryan frowned.

"We'd better head for the tomb," Batman said.

They headed around the base of the hills until they came to a wide hole in the rock.

"This is it," Batman said.

They cautiously made their way inside the pitch-black cave. Batman reached for a flashlight, but Ryan stopped him.

"Look, Batman," he said, pointing.

An eerie, green glow shone from deeper inside the cave. They swiftly and silently moved toward it.

Three glowing, green bubbles floated there. Larry was trapped inside one of the bubbles, his face frozen in a mask of fear. Two other men were trapped in the other bubbles.

"Ectoplasm," Batman said. "Gentleman Ghost is behind this."

Batman took a laser gun from his utility belt. "A blast of Nth energy should take care of this."

He quickly zapped each of the ectoplasm bubbles with a beam of blue light. The bubbles exploded, spraying green slime around the cave. Larry and the two men dropped to the floor.

Larry opened his eyes. He looked dazed. "Ryan?" he asked. "And *Batman*?"

Batman and Ryan helped get the men back to the trailer. They cleaned themselves up and had some hot tea.

"Thanks for saving us, Batman," Larry

said. "I thought we'd never get out of there."

"Gentleman Ghost did this to you," Batman said. "If we're going to find him, I'll need some information from you."

Larry nodded. "Anything you want."

"First, tell me about this Ombos," Batman said.

"We don't know much, but we do know he was a priest in ancient Egypt," Larry explained. "A priest of Set, the god of death and the underworld."

Batman and Ryan exchanged glances. Gentleman Ghost was a criminal who had once made a deal with a demon. He was doomed to live forever—as a ghost. He didn't like that idea one bit, and he longed for the day when the dead would one day rule the earth.

"The probability is high that Gentleman Ghost wants to use Ombos to harness the power of Set," Ryan said.

"Exactly," Batman agreed. "We need to find him fast, before he does. Larry, do you have a map of the area? Are there any other caves or tombs?"

"Sure," Larry said. He spun around and typed into a computer keyboard. A map appeared on the screen. "There's an old abandoned tomb about twenty kilometers from here. Robbers plucked it clean hundreds of years ago."

"Sounds like a good place for a hideout," Batman said. He nodded to Ryan. "We should get there right away."

"Thanks again," Larry said. "But I gotta know one thing. Ryan—how do *you* know Batman? You've always got your face buried in a book or you're working on some new experiment. I mean, you're not exactly the type to hang out with super heroes."

Ryan smiled. It was important for him to keep his hero identity safe—even from an old friend.

"You could say that Batman and I have similar interests," he replied.

CHAPTER
FOUR

It didn't take long to find the tomb
Larry had pointed out on the map. Batman
landed the jet, and the two heroes stepped
out onto the sand. Batman eyed the
narrow tomb opening.

"It won't be easy to get in there without
being detected," he said. "We may lose the
element of surprise."

"As you know, that is not a problem for
me," Ryan told him.

Ryan pressed his belt buckle. The air
around him crackled as waves of atomic
energy surrounded him. Ryan instantly
transformed into the Atom. A skintight,
blue and red costume covered his body
and masked his face. The center of the
gold belt around his waist bore the symbol
of an atom—three electron orbits with a

nucleus in the center.

Electrons circled his body, forming white, shining loops around him. The Atom grew smaller and smaller in front of Batman's eyes until he was no larger than a common ant.

"Turn on your transmitter," Batman instructed. "I'll listen in. Once we find out what Gentlemen Ghost is up to, we'll make our move."

The Atom flew inside the tomb. It was

as dark as the tomb of Ombos, but the energy sparking around the Atom lit his way. He followed a long, twisting passage that opened up into a round chamber lit with torches. Gentleman Ghost floated in the center of the room. Next to him stood a mummy—and it was alive!

The Atom hid in a crack in the stone wall and observed the scene for a moment, fascinated. He could see right through the body of Gentleman Ghost. The villain had no human form, only the clothes he had worn when he died: a cape with a high collar over a waistcoat and pants, boots, and a top hat. The lens of a monocle floated where his eye should have been. In his left hand, he carried a walking stick topped with a grinning skull.

The mummy, on the other hand, appeared to be made of flesh—dried out, leathery flesh. Bandages brown with age were wrapped around most of his body, but the ancient fabric had come loose in some places. The bandages around his face

revealed one red eye and a mouth filled with crooked teeth. Around his neck, he wore a medallion with the face of what looked like an Egyptian god. It was some kind of animal, with a long snout and tall ears.

"I am your liberator, Ombos!" Gentleman Ghost cried. "Thanks to me, you have been freed from your eternal prison. In return, I ask you this favor."

Gentleman Ghost unrolled a scroll. It showed an image of the same Egyptian god, along with hieroglyphic writing.

"Only you can help me to bring back Set, the ancient god of the underworld," Gentleman Ghost said. "Tomorrow night, under the dark moon, Set will rise again. The world will plunge into darkness—and the dead will rule!"

Through the transmitter, Batman heard Gentleman Ghost cackle. He had heard enough.

Batman raced into the tunnel and burst into the chamber. Gentleman Ghost swirled around, startled.

"Batman!" he cried. "Curses!"

He aimed the end of his walking stick at Batman, but Batman was too fast. He took a shooter from his utility belt and sent a pair of purple, glowing handcuffs flying through the air. The handcuffs attached to Gentleman Ghost's sleeves, and his walking stick fell to the chamber floor.

The Atom grew back to his human size and stood next to Batman.

"Nth metal," Batman explained. "The only material that can capture ghosts."

Gentleman Ghost laughed. "Don't be so sure, Batman," he said. He turned to the mummy. "Ombos!"

Ombos began to chant in a low voice in some strange, ancient language. A red light poured from the Set medallion on his chest. The light struck the Nth metal cuffs, and they clattered to the floor.

"Sorry to disappoint you, Batman," Gentleman Ghost said. "But with Ombos by my side, I can't be stopped!"

CHAPTER
FIVE

"We have to split them up," Batman told the Atom.

"Yes," agreed his friend.

The Atom charged across the floor of the tomb.

Pow! He slammed Ombos with an energy-charged atomic punch. The mummy flew backward, colliding with the wall.

Batman threw an Nth metal Batarang at Gentleman Ghost. The villain raised his walking stick and the mouth of the grinning skull opened wide. Purple flames shot out, hitting the Batarang. The weapon clattered harmlessly to the ground.

Gentleman Ghost aimed the purple flames at Batman. He dodged out of the way just in time, somersaulting across the floor.

On the other side of the tomb, the Atom lifted Ombos from the ground. The mummy's medallion glowed again, surrounding the Atom with red light. The Atom pushed against the walls of light around him, but couldn't break through.

Batman threw an Nth lasso around Gentleman Ghost, capturing him. But Ombos chanted the strange incantation again.

Zap! Another beam of red light hit the Nth lasso, and the ropes disintegrated. Gentleman Ghost sent another wave of burning purple flame at Batman. He quickly held up a shield to block the blast.

"Perhaps a negative charge will dissipate this energy," the Atom guessed. He pressed the atom symbol on his belt and an atomic-sized laser gun shot out. Then it grew to normal size. The Atom adjusted the controls and blasted the red-energy prison.

It worked! He flew toward Ombos and slammed him with another powerful punch.

Gentleman Ghost whirled around and aimed a blast of flame at the Atom. The Atom quickly shrunk to avoid the attack.

"Ombos! Call on the army of the dead!" Gentleman Ghost cried.

The mummy groaned and climbed to his feet. A tornado of red light swirled from the medallion this time. When the light faded, a crowd of ghostly figures filled the chamber. Each of the ancient Egyptian warriors wore a loincloth and carried a

spear made of the red, glowing energy.

"Attack!" Gentleman Ghost cried.

Batman heard the Atom in his ear.

"Batman! The tunnel behind you! We must hurry!" he urged.

Batman disliked the idea of running farther into the cave, but they needed a quick way to avoid the onslaught of spears. He raced into the tunnel with the Atom flying by his side.

The tunnel emptied out into another chamber.

"We're trapped," Batman said. He faced the cave's entrance. "We'll have to fight them off."

The Atom grew back to normal size. "The odds are against us."

"Right, but we've got one thing going for us," Batman said. "We're alive."

"Not for long, Batman!"

Gentleman Ghost and Ombos suddenly appeared in the chamber. Gentleman Ghost raised his walking stick—but he pointed it at the chamber entrance.

"How about a tomb for two?" he asked. Cackling, he blasted the entrance with purple flame. The chamber rumbled as the rocks around the entrance caved in, blocking it.

The skull's mouth opened up again, and a purple vortex formed in the chamber. Gentleman Ghost jumped into the vortex.

"Come, Ombos," Gentleman Ghost cried. "Tomorrow the world will be ours!"

The mummy followed him, and the vortex swallowed them up.

CHAPTER SIX

"Where have they gone?" the Atom asked.

"Somewhere we can't follow," Batman said. "The underworld."

Batman aimed his laser gun at the rocks blocking the entrance. The Atom put a hand on his arm.

"There is a high probability that another blast will cause the cave walls to collapse," the Atom said. "I will go for help. Larry should have the proper equipment to extract you safely."

"Thanks, Atom," Batman said.

The Atom shrank to the size of an atomic particle and flew through the cracks in the piled-up rocks. A few hours later, Batman heard the sound of a drill. Larry and Ryan soon excavated a hole large enough for Batman to crawl through.

"Thanks," Batman said. "I was starting to feel like a mummy."

They left the tomb and made their way back to Larry's camp by the tomb of Ombos. The sun was beginning to set. Larry and his two assistants made a fire, and cooked up a meal of canned chili. Ryan and Batman joined them around the fire.

"Gentleman Ghost is going to cast his deadly spell tomorrow night," Batman said.

"We have approximately twenty-four hours to stop him," Ryan added.

"But how?" Larry asked. "Your Nth metal tools are not effective against Ombos's power."

"That's a problem," Batman agreed. "Gentleman Ghost has powerful forces of darkness on his side. In Egyptian mythology, only Ra, the god of the sun, could defeat Set. It's too bad we don't have Ra on our side."

"It's funny that you say that," Larry said. "There's a tomb on the other side of the hill. It's said to contain the body of Ra-Helios, a pharaoh who was said to be the reincarnation of Ra."

"That's convenient, but I don't have the power to bring ancient gods to life," Batman replied.

Larry's two assistants looked at each other. They had been mostly silent all night, awed by the presence of Batman.

"But maybe you do, Batman," said Khai, a slim man with bushy, dark hair.

"It's true," added the other assistant, Adjo. "Legend says that one who carries the light of the sun within can harness the power of Ra."

"A champion," Khai said. "Like you."

Ryan frowned. "This is just a story. There must be a scientific way to defeat Gentleman Ghost."

"Before tonight, I'd never seen a mummy come to life," Batman pointed out. "We can work on strengthening the Nth metal tonight. Tomorrow morning, we'll head for the tomb of Ra-Helios."

"I'll go with you," Larry suggested.

Ryan glanced at Batman.

"Ryan and I can handle this by ourselves," Batman said. "It's better to have you here at camp. If we need help, we'll contact you."

"Sure," Larry said, but he sounded disappointed—and a little jealous. Ryan was grateful to Batman for helping to keep his secret.

Ryan and Batman set up a makeshift

lab and worked on the Nth metal that night. They slept for a few hours and woke up before sunrise. Then they climbed into Batman's jet. Ryan transformed into the Atom, and they headed for the tomb of Ra-Helios.

The tomb entrance looked like all of the others: a hole carved into the rocky hillside. When they stepped inside, they saw a huge stone wall a few feet in. The wall was covered with hieroglyphs.

"I can read every symbol on the periodic table of elements, but I can't read hieroglyphs," the Atom said.

"I spent some time in Egypt during my training," Batman said. He took a step forward. He felt the stone under his foot give under the pressure.

"Batman!"

The footstep had triggered a trap door in the ceiling. The ceiling opened up, and hundreds of green, wriggling snakes rained down on their heads!

"It's a booby trap!" the Atom yelled.

CHAPTER
SEVEN

Batman quickly jumped back. He plucked a can from his utility belt and sprayed it in the cave.

An icy wind shot from the can. The slithering snakes stopped moving completely, freezing like statues.

"A little cold should chill out these reptiles," Batman said.

"Good thinking, Batman," the Atom said. "Some of these snakes appear to be poisonous. The first colony was most likely placed here when the tomb was first built, as a way to keep out intruders."

"They'll warm up soon," Batman said. "We should try to get inside this tomb."

As he spoke, the first rays of morning sunlight shone inside the cave. They lit up the wall of hieroglyphs.

"What does it say, Batman?" the Atom asked.

"This wall is a door," Batman said. He took an X-ray scanner from his utility belt and aimed it at the door. "Take a look at this."

The X-ray showed a complicated maze inside the door. Different pathways were blocked with what looked like springs and pieces of metal.

"The whole door is one big locking

mechanism," Batman said. He pointed to a gold disk in the center of the wall. There were tiny marks engraved around it, making it look like the dial of a combination lock. "That's the handle. It can open the door, but if you turn it the wrong way, or the wrong number of times, it will activate more booby traps."

"I think I can solve this puzzle," the Atom said.

He shrunk down to the size of an atomic particle and flew inside the door through a narrow opening around the gold disk. Then he darted through the maze, taking each and every turn. He could see which paths led to booby traps, and which paths would unlock the door. Then he used his strength to push down the correct levers one by one.

Batman watched as the gold disk spun and clicked in front of him. Then the heavy stone door slid to the side. The Atom flew back out and returned to his normal size.

"Nice job," Batman said.

The Atom grinned. "They say that solving puzzles strengthens brain function."

The two men entered the tomb. The morning sunlight traveled down the corridor and hit a copper mirror. The light reflected down a passage to the right.

"Looks like we should follow the sun," Batman said.

They made their way through the tomb, following the bending light to a small chamber. The walls were covered with polished copper, and sunlight bounced off of them, filling the chamber with a bright glow.

The chamber contained a stone sarcophagus with a gold lid. Carved into the lid was the face of a pharaoh wearing a round disk on his head shaped like the sun. Images of falcons, the symbol of Ra, were engraved in the stone coffin. A message in hieroglyphs was written at the pharaoh's feet.

"When darkness falls, Ra will rise again,"

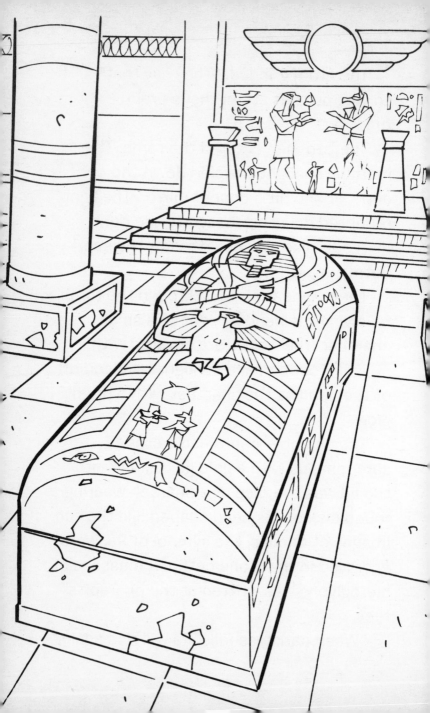

Batman read. "One who is filled with the light of the sun shall call, and Ra will answer."

"Khai and Adjo were right," the Atom said.

"I'm a crime fighter, not a saint," Batman said.

"You are a champion of justice," his friend pointed out. "It is probable that this is what the pharaoh had in mind."

Batman placed both hands on the sarcophagus. "Might as well try," he said. He read aloud the words on the sarcophagus.

The gold lid of the sarcophagus shone like bright sunlight. The figure of the pharaoh rose from the coffin. He hovered in the air, shimmering before them.

A deep, powerful voice filled the minds of the two heroes.

"Who has awakened Ra-Helios?"

Batman bowed respectfully.

"We need your help, mighty pharaoh," Batman said. "Ombos, the priest of Set, has been released from his tomb. A spirit from the underworld, Gentleman Ghost, plans to use Ombos to resurrect Set and cast the world in eternal darkness."

The pharaoh nodded gravely. Once again, Batman and the Atom heard his voice in their minds.

"If Ombos succeeds, then the world will be in peril," Ra-Helios said. "Ages ago, I battled Set as Ra, god of the sun. I was nearly overcome by his dark forces, but the greatest sorcerers in the land created a powerful weapon—the staff of Ra. With the staff, I banished Set to the underworld."

The pharaoh held out his right hand. A golden staff topped with a sun disk appeared in his hand. The staff transformed from an object made of shimmering, ghostly matter into a weapon of solid gold before their eyes.

"Tonight is the night of the dark moon," Ra-Helios said. "Ombos will need to perform his magic at the temple of Set in Amshir."

The pharaoh held out his left hand and gave each of them a small, gold talisman. Each one was inscribed with the image of a falcon.

"Hold these and call my name," Ra-Helios told them. "I will join your battle and defeat Set with my staff."

Batman bowed again. "Thank you, Ra-Helios."

The shimmering vision of the pharaoh disappeared. The tomb went dark. No sunlight reflected from the copper walls.

Puzzled, Batman and the Atom ran out of the tomb. Outside, they saw the last rays of the sun disappear behind the horizon. They had only been in the tomb for a short time, but already night was falling.

"It's possible that time inside the tomb flows on a different time stream than outside the tomb," the Atom guessed.

"Good hypothesis," Batman agreed. "Or else Gentleman Ghost and Ombos have figured out a way to make nightfall come faster so we can't stop them. Either way, we've got to hurry!"

"Right," the Atom agreed.

They climbed into the jet. Batman set the coordinates for the temple of Set.

The sky grew darker and darker as they flew. As they neared Amshir, they saw a temple made of black marble. Stone columns supported the ceiling, which opened up at the top to reveal the sanctuary inside. Below, Ombos and Gentleman Ghost stood around a flaming brass bowl.

Batman programmed the jet for an automatic landing.

"This looks like a good time to drop in," he said.

The Atom nodded. They opened the jet doors and jumped. Batman's cape acted like a parachute, setting him down safely on the floor next to Gentleman Ghost. The Atom crackled with energy as he landed next to Ombos.

"You're too late, Batman," Gentleman

Ghost said. "The mighty Set has risen! Darkness will rule the world!"

As Gentleman Ghost spoke, the sand in front of the temple began to stir. A large figure rose from the desert floor—a dark creature with the body of a man and the face of a strange beast with long ears and long, black hair. He carried a spear topped with the head of a vulture.

The Atom glanced at Batman. He nodded, and they each held up their talisman.

"Ra-Helios!" they shouted.

The glowing form of Ra-Helios, as large and powerful as Set, appeared in front of the temple. He pointed the golden staff at Set.

"Return to your prison, Lord of Darkness!" Ra-Helios cried.

Suddenly, a glowing, purple grappling hook swung from the ceiling of the temple. It gripped the staff of Ra and swung it toward Gentleman Ghost.

The villain held up his walking stick and created another vortex to the underworld.

The staff of Ra disappeared inside the vortex.

Gentleman Ghost cackled with glee. "Thank you, Batman," he said. "You've led Ra-Helios right into my trap!"

CHAPTER
NINE

"And you shall feel my wrath!" Ra-Helios boomed.

A jagged bolt of golden lightning shot from his fingertips and slammed into Gentleman Ghost, knocking the walking stick from the villian's hand.

Then Ra-Helios cried out in pain and surprise as a stream of black light from Set's staff hit him in the back. He spun around to face his old rival.

"I do not need my staff to defeat you!" he cried. He hurled bolts of golden light at Set. At the same time, Set sent black light shooting from his staff. The light and darkness met, the forces pushing against each other.

Gentleman Ghost was still too weak to get up. "Ombos! Raise the army!" he yelled.

The mummy nodded and began to utter the ancient chant. One by one, the ghostly warriors appeared behind him.

The Atom's fists began to glow. "A negative charge worked before. It is highly probable that it will work again," he told Batman. Then he tested out his theory.

Pow! He slammed a fist into the nearest warrior. The ghost popped like a soap bubble.

Batman set his laser gun to produce a

negative-energy blast. "Good idea!"

Pow! Pow! Pow! The Atom punched warrior after warrior, taking them all down.

Zap! Zap! Zap! Each blast of energy from Batman's weapon evaporated one of the warriors.

"No!" Gentleman Ghost wailed. He slowly floated off of the floor. He spotted his walking stick and raced toward it.

But Batman was quicker. He shot a hooked line from his utility belt and pulled the staff away before Gentleman Ghost could reach it.

Down on the sand, the battle raged between Ra-Helios and Set. Both gods strained to keep up the flow of energy. Every time Set's attack got stronger, Ra-Helios countered with a powerful burst of golden light, but it still wasn't enough to overpower Set. Batman knew he needed the staff of Ra to win the battle.

He looked down at the staff in his hand and got an idea. He moved it in a circle, just as he had seen Gentleman Ghost do.

The skull's mouth opened, and out came a swirling purple vortex—a gateway to the underworld.

Batman pulled a strong line from his utility belt and tossed it to the Atom. His friend had finished off the last warrior.

"Don't let go," Batman said.

Then he dove inside the Vortex.

"Grab the line!" Gentleman Ghost cried.

He and Ombos lunged at the Atom. He quickly shrank to the size of an atom—but kept his full human strength. The Atom kept a tight grip on the line and quickly flew around the heads of the ghost and the mummy. They tried to grab the end of the line, but the Atom was just too fast.

Batman emerged from the vortex just in time, pulling himself up with the rope. He held Gentleman Ghost's staff in one hand— and the gleaming staff of Ra in the other.

Ombos tackled Batman. Before he hit the floor, Batman threw the staff like a spear.

"Ra-Helios, this belongs to you!"

Batman called out.

The sun god grabbed the staff in his right hand. Then he held it high above his head.

"Return to the darkness!" he cried.

He brought the glowing staff down on Set. The god's body slowly filled with Ra's glowing light.

Boom! Set exploded. Drops of black rain poured down on the temple.

Bam! The Atom, now back to his human size, punched Ombos, sending him flying off of Batman.

Batman jumped up and slapped a pair of Nth metal cuffs on Gentleman Ghost.

"These stronger cuffs should be magic-proof," Batman said.

"In case they are not, I have taken a precaution," said the Atom. He had tied a strip of mummy cloth securely around Ombos's mouth.

Ra-Helios turned to the temple. He touched the staff of Ra to the mummy's head.

"Return to your tomb," said the sun god.

Ombos slowly faded away.

"Thank you, Ra-Helios," Batman said. "You've saved us all."

"I suppose you'll want to rule the world yourself now," Gentleman Ghost said, sounding like an angry child.

"I rule the daylight, as Set still rules the darkness," Ra-Helios said. "There must be balance in the world. Equal amounts of darkness and light. Like you, Batman. You fashion yourself as a creature of the night, but inside, you shine with the brightness of the sun. I must thank you for being such a faithful warrior."

Batman bowed his head. "It has been an honor."

Gentleman Ghost snorted. "Oh, please!"

Then Ra-Helios slowly faded, leaving only the stars glowing in the dark night sky.

CHAPTER
TEN

Larry freaked out a little when Batman and Ryan showed up in the jet—with Gentleman Ghost secured in the backseat.

"Is that really a . . . ghost?" Larry asked nervously.

"Not just *any* ghost," Gentleman Ghost called from the jet. "The most brilliant criminal mind in existence, living or dead!"

Larry looked at Ryan. "I thought you didn't believe in ghosts?"

Ryan shrugged. "In this case, I cannot ignore the evidence."

"The rest of your dig should go smoothly," Batman said. "Ombos is back in his tomb."

Larry shuddered. "I'm not sure if I want to go back in there. I'm thinking of taking up botany instead," he said. "But I really need to thank you, Batman. You, too, Ryan.

I always thought you were kind of a wimp.
You must be pretty tough if you're hanging
out with Batman."

"He is," Batman agreed. "And now
we've got to head back to Gotham City.
Gentleman Ghost has a nice Nth metal cell
waiting for him there."

"You won't be able to hold me there for

long, Batman!" Gentleman Ghost cried.

Ryan looked at Batman. "Do you have a music player in your jet? I think it will be a very long trip if we have to listen to Gentleman Ghost all the way home."

Batman grinned. "We'll turn the volume way up."

They climbed into the jet just as a beeping sound came from Batman's helmet—another message. He listened carefully.

"Feel like making a stop in Paris?" he asked. "Someone is robbing the art museums there."

"Considering that we just defeated a mummy, a ghost, and a god of darkness, there is a high probability that catching an art thief will be a piece of cake," Ryan answered.

Batman smiled. "There's one thing I've learned—when you're fighting for justice, *anything* can happen."

The jet's engines roared to life, and they sped off to greet another adventure.

12-10